ORLANDO THE ARCHER

&

The Princess of the Four Winds

by
Edward Eriksson
Illustrated by:

This book dedicated to

Evan

Kristian

Dimitri

Bryan

Lili

Michaela

Michael

Harry

Matthew

Wyatt

and

Alice

ORLANDO THE ARCHER

&

The Princess of the Four Winds

1

Once upon a time when kings ruled in many lands, a young man went out to hunt in the forest. His name was Orlando, and he carried a bow and a quiver of arrows slung over his shoulder. Early one morning he left his cottage, hoping to find a bear or a wild pig to shoot and bring home to his mother for food. All day he walked and stopped and crept and looked. But the woods, it seemed, were empty; and now it grew dark, and suddenly he realized he was lost.

Fortunately, a big round moon shone brightly, and Orlando found his way to a clearing, where in the distance he saw the moon hanging just above the treetops. As one way looked as good as another, he decided to walk toward the moon since that way there would be some light falling on his path. He went about a mile before the moon disappeared, blocked from view by a huge dark mound. But the mound had a light glowing at its base; a light, Orlando noticed as he got closer, coming from a cave.

"What luck," he thought. "Maybe I'll find a welcome here."

He looked for a place to knock, but finding none he started to enter, when he was frightened

three steps back by the dark figure of an old woman.

"Stop!" commanded the figure, holding up a warning hand. She had a hollow, quivering voice. She wore a long dark cloak with a hood that covered part of her face, but Orlando was struck by her long nose and chin and her bright blue eyes that glowed in the dark. "Are you prepared to serve?" she asked.

"I don't know," answered the young man, who wondered what the dark figure meant. Did serving mean waiting on tables, chopping wood, digging in salt mines? "I'm lost, ma'am, uh . . . " he began as offering an excuse. "I'm also tired and hungry. I've been walking all day in the forest."

"You'll be fed," the words came quivering and hollow. "But you may not enter." Orlando could not see the figure's mouth; it was deep in the hood's shadow. But within the hood the two eyes burned with a strange blue luster. "This is the Cave of Hidden Light," explained the voice. "Do you know how you found it?"

"I followed the moon," said Orlando.

"Ah," said the strange woman. "Exactly. Here we put to service all who are lost and follow the moon. Here we teach you to follow something more mysterious than the moon. Here we teach you to follow the Hidden Light. If you do, you will find happiness. But first you must be prepared to work, to use your imagination, and to be adventurous."

Hesitating, Orlando finally said, "I'm a hunter: I know most of the forest." If he was going to have to work, he wanted to put in a preference for the great outdoors. Naturally, he was prepared to use his imagination and go on adventures.

"It's a small forest," said the woman. "Can you ride a horse?"

"I could try," offered the lad.

"Here," said the hooded creature, extending a thin hand with a small cake. "Eat this." Once Orlando had taken, chewed, and swallowed it, the woman announced: "Now you must travel to the moon!"

"The moon!" exclaimed the young man, swallowing once more. "Why? I mean, how?"

"Why?" repeated the dark creature. "Because I want you to go on a mission to bring some horses to the King of the Eastern Hills. How, you will learn. Are you willing?"

The young hunter thought a while. He imagined that there would be danger on such an errand. But would it be any worse than spending the night cold and tired in a weird part of the forest? He suddenly felt stronger now that he had eaten, for the little cake gave him a lot of energy; and besides, he thought, it would be interesting to learn how to travel up to the moon. He nodded to the dark figure. Yes, he would go.

"Here," said the mysterious shape, reaching out to Orlando. "Turn around, and don't be afraid." As the young man turned, the creature grabbed hold of his quiver of arrows, charging it with a glow of light. "Take an arrow now," ordered the voice. "Put it to your bow, and shoot it over this mound, the Mound of Ancient Earth."

Orlando did as commanded. The arrow soared upward into the darkness. And trailing behind it was a wide ribbon of golden light extending beautifully above the lad like a radiant pathway into the nighttime sky.

"Follow it!" ordered the voice.

Orlando, as soon as he heard, felt himself lifted into the air and drawn bodily along the ribbon of golden light, past the highest trees, far above the Mound of Ancient Earth, higher and higher, through wisps of clouds, into the cold night air. As he ascended, he saw the moon grow larger and larger. He turned and saw the globe of earth grow smaller and smaller. Still he glided upward.

"This feels great!" he shouted.

Soon all he saw before him was the yellow moon, wider than a mountain. And soon he landed, standing on red moon dust in front of a corral fence. Beyond, he saw a house; and so he jumped over the fence and walked to the house, supposing (correctly, of course) that this was the first step on his mission. Orlando did not think it too strange to find a house with a corral fence on the moon, since he lived during

the time before science was taught and even before Galileo invented the telescope—so he was prepared for anything. Nor did he think it strange to see a man with a big bald head humming to himself as he rocked to and fro on a rocking chair on the porch of the house. Or was he giggling? Or was he humming and giggling at the same time?

"This must be the Man in the Moon," thought Orlando.

"Right you are! The Man in the Moon!" shouted the bald-headed fellow, rising and startling the young adventurer, who suddenly noticed that the moon was a very quiet place, where even thoughts could be heard. The Man in the Moon rose and shook Orlando's hand. "And you're here about the horses." He gave a wild, neighing kind of laugh, but his head was so very round and so very bald that he seemed more jolly than crazy, and the lad was relieved to know that he didn't have to offer the gentleman a complicated explanation.

"I'm good at guessing," the bald fellow winked. Then he whistled, and out from the barn at the side of the house galloped twelve handsome horses, who stopped in a semi-circle around Orlando and the man. Three of the horses were white, three were light brown, three were dark brown, and three were dapple gray. The man whistled again, and suddenly amidst a swirl of moon dust, he and his horses rose from the ground and perched above the mass of cloud created by the swirling dust.

"These are Moon Horses," said the Man in the Moon with a sweep of his hand. "I call them Months." He looked at the young man with a sly smile. "Get it?" He laughed a slow, throaty laugh.

Orlando had grown up at the forest's edge. In fact, he had not gone to school for very long; so he had never heard of months. Time did pass for him, but one day, to his mind, was like the next. Even so, he did not want to seem stupid; so he merely shrugged his shoulders and decided to think while the Man in the Moon talked.

"January, February," these were two white horses; "March, April, May," were light brown; "June, July, August," were dark brown; "September, October November," were dapple gray; "and December," was the other white one. All were introduced to Orlando.

"So my job is to deliver these Moon Horses . . ." he began but was interrupted.

"To the King of the Eastern Hills. Do you want to know why?"

"Yes, of course," said Orlando.

"Because he needs the time," answered the bald-headed fellow. "In fact, he needs one whole year."

"For what?" asked the lad.

The Man in the Moon only nodded and laughed strangely. He motioned for the young man to lead off the Moon Horses—"The Months," said Orlando quietly to himself—and then he and the horses floated back down to the moon-ground.

Orlando felt uncomfortable leading the horses over the red moon dust out of the corral fence, because he wasn't sure how to get them back down to earth. But the Man in the Moon answered his thoughts, for the lad heard an eerie voice behind him in the distance.

"Sho-o-o-ot your arro-o-o-ow!"

So he did, and the arrow traveled in an arc out beyond the moon, and trailing behind it was the wide ribbon of golden light. Orlando was lifted above the red moon dust, and the horses followed behind him in single file: first January, then February, and the rest in order, March, April, May, June, July, August, September, October, November, and finally December. Out into space they glided, across the wide gap between the earth and the moon, then into the atmosphere, and down past clouds, down, down, down, below the mountains, below the trees, landing softly in a forest clearing. And since the journey took all night, no sooner had they touched the ground than the sun rose over the Eastern Hills and morning light chased the darkness from the land.

2

Orlando looked about the clearing, expecting to see the strange figure from the Cave of Hidden Light; when no one appeared, he sat on a rock in the middle of the clearing, and with his head propped in his hand, elbow on knee, he gazed at the twelve horses from the moon—the Months—standing in a semi-circle around him as they did when he first met them. What should he do now?

The horses were supposed to be delivered to the King of the Eastern Hills. But where did he live? And who was he? And why did he need the horses? Because he needed the time? Just then Orlando noticed the red morning sun rising above the distant hills, and he had an answer to his first question.

"The sun," he said to himself, "always rises in the east, over the Eastern Hills, and that is where I'm likely to find the king!" Orlando, you see, used his imagination.

So off he went, towards the rising sun, the horses following in a line as he rode on the first Moon Horse, January. (The horse had volunteered by kneeling so that the young man, who had never ridden before, could mount him; and by now the youth realized that all he needed was a good attitude and the horses would follow his direction.) He rode for most of the morning, stopping once by a woodland stream, to allow the horses to rest

and have a drink. When the sun was almost at its zenith (that is, the topmost part of the sky), he found himself at the base of an enormous hill, different from the other, surrounding hills in that these were covered with greenery; but this one, the tallest, was completely bare of tree or bush, being brown and dusty. At the base of this awesome sight sat the large figure of an old man with red hair and red beard; he wore a long red robe lined with gray fur, but it was soiled and torn; and the king (for Orlando knew it must be the king, as he wore a golden crown) sat with his head in both hands, looking gloomily at the ground. As the lad approached, he looked up but said nothing.

"I've brought the Moon Horses," explained Orlando. "The Months. The Man in the Moon said you needed them; or rather he said you needed the time."

The king rose silently and inspected each of the horses. He checked their teeth and slapped their flanks. Then he sighed.

"Nice," he said, "but they won't do much good. The winds keep blowing." He stretched his hand upward to the top of the hill. Orlando's eyes followed the movement to where he saw for an instant, like a crown on its top, a castle wall. Then the view was spoiled by gusts of wind blowing this way and that, making loud, eerie noises, and ruffling up the dirt in blinding clouds.

"My daughter's up there!" began the king, whose eyes bulged as he shouted louder and louder. He looked as if he was going crazy. But he had to shout to be heard above the noisy wind. "I can't get to her! I need steps! The hill was once green! And now . . . !" It wasn't green anymore. "The winds came and blew all the trees and bushes away! I'd been out hunting, and when I came back everything was bare, and there was the princess trapped high up on this barren hill!"

The old king took a deep breath and dropped into his chair. He sat looking gloomily at the ground. The wind subsided.

"You need steps?" asked Orlando.

"Yes," replied the king without looking up, "and if you can get me up to her or get her down to me, why, you can marry her."

"But I'm just a poor hunter," said the lad.

"And I'm a rich king," answered the old

reddish-haired, red-bearded fellow. "But rich or poor, no one can be anything to her while the princess is trapped up there." He spoke with a wide-eyed stare. He was desperate.

Orlando thought it would be pretty nice to be married to a king's daughter, for then he too would be rich as a king and would not need to go hunting every day for his food.

"There are stones all around," said the unhappy king with a toss of his hand; and indeed there were, since hundreds of them had tumbled down the hill when the winds had blown.

The young man then went straight to work. He harnessed January with ropes the king had used when trying to climb the hill without steps, and he began to set the stones into the hillside. But the work went slowly and was doubly hard

because the winds were up again, and they blew icy and strong. Then the first horse tired. So Orlando harnessed February. After a while, this horse also tired, and the youth harnessed the next one, March.

But as he worked with March, the winds blew stronger and stronger until he felt he would never get the steps even half way up the hill. He sat next to the king, unhappy and exhausted.

"I'll never get this job done," he said.

"Probably not," agreed the king, who had been too miserable to help. "You can't fight magic."

"Magic?" asked Orlando.

"Of course it's magic," said the king. "Didn't I tell you?"

"No."

"I guess I should have," said the king. "But I've just got too much on my mind to think of everything."

"What kind of magic?" asked Orlando.

"Strong stuff," said the king, shaking his red-bearded head. "The Wizard of the Crystal Lake—he's a nasty guy—well, he wanted to marry Rosalinda, the princess, my daughter. Well, I said no. Why? Because he was too frosty and mean. If he came close to you, he'd give you chills one day and you'd have a fever the next. He could walk through a garden and kill flowers just by breathing on them. Not somebody you'd want hanging around the castle."

As he spoke the winds blew wildly about the hillside.

"Isn't there a way to fight this magic?" asked Orlando.

After a moment's silence the king suggested, "You could try Father Time."

"Where can I find him?" asked the young man.

The old king shook his red-bearded head. "That's not so easy," he said. "Father Time lives in the sun."

"I've been to the moon," said the young archer gallantly. "I suppose I could go to the sun."

"The sun is a lot farther away than the moon," replied the old king wisely.

But Orlando had already placed an arrow in his bow, and aiming it directly at the sun as it began to set in the west, he pulled back as hard as he could and let the arrow fly. Up and away it soared, straight towards the setting sun; and as it sped, a wide ribbon of golden light lengthened out behind it.

Then the lad felt himself lifted from the ground and carried forward into the reddening western sky.

3

The air was cooler higher up as Orlando glided above the clouds, colored pink by the setting sun. Soon he sailed beyond the clouds, soaring wonderfully farther and farther away from the earth. Then before he was halfway on his journey, he began to slow up, and soon he barely moved. Then he stopped midway between the earth and the sun, where the earth seemed small and far away and the sun loomed large and golden before him. Wondering what had happened, he noticed a speck in the distance traveling towards him from the sun.

The speck grew until it became a blot; then the blot become a large silhouette, and this finally became an old man with a scraggly beard. He wore a gray robe and held a scythe, (which is a tool with a curved blade at the end of a long wooden handle).

"Where do you think you're going?" he asked Orlando.

"To the sun," said the youth.

"I wouldn't If I were you," said the old man, who was indeed Father Time. "It's too hot there. Trust me, better stop here."

"Well," said the young man, who had mixed feelings about stopping in the middle of nowhere. The sun probably was too hot, but how long could he stay here standing on nothing? "I have a problem."

"If I can help, I will," said Father Time, smiling kindly through missing teeth. "In fact, I saw you coming. Speak. Now is as good a time as any."

So Orlando, poised between the small blue earth and the huge yellow sun, told Father Time the story of the Moon Horses and the King of the Eastern Hills and of Rosalinda and the Wizard of the Crystal Lake.

"That's a very sad story," said the old man, as a tear rolled down his cheek past a wart on his nose. "Time was when I could have married a princess. But, alas." He had a faraway look in his eyes.

"I'm sorry," said the young hunter.

"No need to be," answered Father Time, wiping the tear, "since that was a long time ago, and I was a younger man." He smiled sadly. "But now I am older and have no need of such stuff. Older and wiser. And I know what you need is a charm."

"Great idea," said Orlando. "Do you have one?"

"I have," replied kindly Father Time, and he waved his arm behind him as if he were gathering air. Suddenly, in his grip was a long leather strap of silver bells, so long it seemed to reach halfway back to earth. "You don't need to count them," said the old magician. "There are 365."

"Wow," said Orlando.

"Divide them among your horses, and as you work, the jangling of the bells will tame the winds." As he said this, Father Time wound up the strap so that the lad could carry it more easily.

"Thanks," said Orlando and asked him how he could repay him, but the gentle old fellow assured him that thanks was payment enough.

He then directed the young man to shoot his arrow towards the earth, and as Orlando started to glide home along the ribbon of golden light, Father Time reached forward and handed him the coiled leather strap of 365 bells.

"Good luck," said the old man, nodding and smiling with watery eyes.

"Thanks again," shouted the lad as he moved forward in the arrow's golden path. Down, down, down, he came.

Soon the sun had set beyond the western

horizon. The clouds were black silhouettes in the evening air. No moon shone as the youth landed in the dark forest, but he found his way back to the king and high hill by the brightness of the many silver bells, glowing with a light taken from the sun.

4

Even the king was impressed by the silver bells. So he and Orlando began immediately to divide them among the horses. Standing by was March, who got 31 bells. Then April got 30. The idea was to give an extra bell to every other Month Horse. So May got 31 bells, June got 30, and July got 31.

"This is going very well," said the king, who enjoyed hanging the bell straps around the horses' necks after the young man counted the bells and cut the leather in the right place. But Orlando lost count as the king spoke, and he cut

31 bells for August. Well, then, September got 30, October 31, November 30, and December 31.

"That's it!" cried the king, who wasn't used to working and became easily tired.

But Orlando corrected him: "We started with March. There are two more horses." In speaking, the young man missed his place and cut 31 bells for January. That left only 28 bells for poor February. Both the king and the helpful archer felt foolish for losing count and short-jangling February.

"Well, that's life," shrugged the king, who was not one for complicated thinking. "Besides, now he won't have to work as long as the others."

And this was true. Happily, the work was completed on December 31st, just in time for a New Year's Eve celebration. The work took a full year for the steps to reach the hilltop castle, as every horse worked for as many days as it had bells.

How did the charm of the bells work?

Well, as long as the horses dragged the stones up the hill and the bells jangled around their necks, no winds blew, and all was calm. The music of the bells tamed the winds. So the work got done.

The scene of the meeting between the king and Princess Rosalinda was full of joy. The princess, who had been left with the entire kitchen staff (among the others who ordinarily lived in the castle) and a great store of food, had ordered a feast prepared as she watched the completion of the stairway up to the castle wall. So there was merriment on New Year's Eve in the hilltop dining hall. And the king said:

"Let's do this every year!" And all the people cheered.

Rosalinda was happy to be engaged to Orlando, who was a handsome fellow, with bright eyes and a pleasant smile; he, for his part, on seeing the princess' beauty, felt the long effort had been worth all his pains. They kissed and pledged their love.

But this is not the end of the story, for that night, the first night of the new year, the Wizard of the Crystal Lake worked his revenge.

5

While everyone in the castle slept, and while the Moon Horses lay still and not a bell sounded in the royal stables, the Wizard of the Crystal Lake caused an icy wind to cover the hillside with a snowy frost. The icy wind came quickly and quietly. It froze everything in the castle. It froze the water in pails and spouts; it froze the food left on the tables and put away in cupboards; it froze the curtains and the clothes and the bed sheets; and then it froze the sleepers, both human and animal, who now lay like icy statues on their beds or on the stable straw. Finally it spread a thick sheet of ice upon the hilltop castle, which now glistened under the starry night like a palace of ice in the frozen North.

Fortunately, there were two who were not frozen. There was Orlando, who was too excited to sleep and who had gotten out of bed to walk around on the castle wall. The exercise kept him warm. And there was Princess Rosalinda, who had arisen in the middle of the night to write in her diary, something she had done every night since being trapped in the castle. She had lit a fire to see by. And so she kept warm. It was Orlando, who, seeing the light in her room, had come with the terrible news: Her father the king and the three friends who had kept her company for a year, the king's ministers, the outdoor staff, all the kitchen help, and all the horses lay frozen stiff where they had fallen asleep. The whole castle had turned into a world of ice.

The princess, who understood a lot about people, realized immediately that the mischief had been done by the Wizard of the Crystal Lake, whose heart was full of envy.

"He was furious when he couldn't marry me," she sighed. "Now he wants no one to be happy."

"He certainly waited for the right moment," said Orlando, whose teeth chattered with cold.

"Lovers don't play fair," commented the princess.

"Where can we find him?" asked her future husband.

"He lives in the frozen North," she answered.

"Then let's go," said Orlando, whose happiness depended on acting swiftly. He strung an arrow and aimed it high in a northerly direction, shooting it over the wind towards the Crystal Lake. Then he held the surprised princess around the waist and the two of them traveled together on the ribbon of golden light. They landed as dawn shone with a pale glow on the sparkling ice forest surrounding Crystal Lake.

Then the wizard arose out of the icy water. He wore a white robe and had icicles dangling from his hair and beard.

"So you've escaped!" he shouted at them from the middle of the lake.

"We have, but you won't," replied Orlando, who had drawn his bow and was ready to let fly an arrow at the nasty man of ice.

"No," insisted the princess. "You can't kill a wizard. Besides, he loved me once."

"Even if you could kill me," cried the horrible wizard, "who would raise the magic spell from your hilltop castle?"

"Is it the princess you want?" shouted Orlando.

"Did I say that?" asked the wizard.

"You can't have her," said the young archer. "I worked for a year to rescue her, and I'm the one she loves."

"Love!" bellowed the icicle-bespangled wizard. "Do I look like someone who does wild things for love?" He certainly looked as if he did wild things, but he didn't look as if he did them for love. "I have other reasons for casting my frozen magic spell."

"Oh, yeah," hollered Orlando. "What?"

"I like to feel my energy," explained the wizard, coming closer and speaking in an ordinary voice. "Something I have a lot of. I mean, winds. Those bells of yours have lulled my winds."

"We had work to do," said the young man.

"And I have winds to blow!" replied the icy wizard, who had reached the lake shore and stood quite close to the other two, chilling the air around them.

"You never wanted to marry the princess?" asked Orlando.

"Well," said the wizard, "that wouldn't have hurt."

"Couldn't we compromise?" suggested Princess Rosalinda, smiling at the wizard. "If we settle this peaceably, I'll seal the bargain with a kiss."

"I'll listen. What do you suggest?" asked the wizard, who hadn't been kissed since the beginning of time.

"Just this," began the princess. "As I stood on the castle wall day after day, watching your terrible winds blow about the hill, I wondered if something couldn't be done to make better use of so much energy."

"I will not tame my winds," cried the nasty wizard.

"I'm not asking you to," said Rosalinda. "My suggestion is for you to make them different. For instance, cold winds from the north are fine in winter when it's fun to play in the ice and snow. But towards the end of February people begin to long for something nicer, like an easterly wind that brings rain for flowers; and then in June we'd like to have warm breezes from the south—they're so relaxing. And then come October, it's time for the wild western winds to blow the leaves from the trees and toss the seeds of wild plants around the earth; and so there would be a time and a season for different kinds of what you call energy."

"Four different winds, eh?" said the wizard, who liked the idea.

"Four winds would be nice," replied the princess.

"Do you agree?" asked the wizard, turning to Orlando.

"Anything the princess wants," said the young man, "is fine with me."

"Then it's a deal," the wizard nodded, and he held before him a crystal pendant offering it to the princess. "You are now the Princess of the Four Winds, and this is a token of our agreement."

"Thank you very much," she said, taking the crystal pendant, "and now will you please raise the icy spell from my father's castle?"

"First," replied the wizard, "your part of the bargain." And he tapped his cheek with a long frosty finger.

"Oh, yes, the kiss," said the tender-hearted Rosalinda, who leaned forward and kissed the wizard on his stone-cold cheek. Her breath was so warm and her kiss so sincere that the wretched wizard, who was mostly made up of ice and snow, melted right in front of the two young people; and as he melted, the spell was lifted from the castle far away on the Eastern Hills, where everyone and everything thawed, returning to normal.

"He's disappeared," cried Orlando.

"Yes," said Rosalinda, "but look." And there

in the distance, in the middle of the Crystal Lake, appeared the wizard as he was before, for ice doesn't stay melted long in the frozen North. The wizard waved goodbye to them and sank into the chilling lake.

6

When the young couple returned to the hilltop castle, everyone was busy chattering about how it felt to be frozen and unfrozen on New Year's Day. Once that stopped, Rosalinda and Orlando sat atop the horse January and paraded about the castle grounds greeting people, who cheered as they passed.

"Oh, Father," cried the princess, kissing the old king, "I'm so glad you're still alive!"

That's when Orlando remembered something. He had left his mother over a year ago in the cottage at the edge of the forest.

"You have a mother?" asked the king. "Why haven't you told us?"

"I had a lot of things to do," said the young hunter, flushing with embarrassment, "first for the old woman from the Cave of Hidden Light and then for you and the princess."

But as happy as he was about his daughter's return, the king didn't think it was good for a lad to be too busy to remember his mother, especially since, as the king discovered, the woman was a widow. He insisted they pay her a visit, and they set off at once.

"I've been keeping this pot of bean and barley soup warm for over a year!" cried Orlando's mother when she found him at the cottage door. "Where have you been?"

"Using my imagination," he said, "going on adventures, and working for the king." He then introduced her to the princess and her father.

"Well," said his mother, who calmed down when she learned that her son had not been in trouble and had instead found respectable work. "Please come in." She was truly happy that Orlando had not gotten mixed up with the wrong people, as she had feared. Instead, he now brought her new relations, of the best sort.

She served the king her bean and barley soup, and the king said it was the tastiest soup he ever eaten. He then asked Orlando's mother to marry him (since his queen had died some years earlier), claiming that so patient a mother would probably make an even better wife. He described the wonderful ceremony that came with a royal wedding.

"But what would I wear?" fretted the old woman.

"Don't worry about that!" said the king, and so she didn't.

The double wedding ceremony came at the end of February. Everyone in the kingdom was invited, and everyone came, bringing gifts and enjoying the food and the music. Even the king's old friends from other lands showed up, full of stories and laughter. It was a jolly occasion. The princess couldn't have been happier. At one point in the festivities, she rose and commanded everyone to be still.

"Thank you all for making this day so happy for me with your gifts and your company. Please stay another day to celebrate our marriages and also to commemorate my reign as Princess of the Four Winds." Then she called forth the horse February, and showing everyone the crystal pendant, the gift of the Wizard of the Crystal Lake, she added it to the 28 bells that hung from his neck.

"This," she said to the horse, "is to give you an extra day this year, for we will have an extra day of feasting. And since there are now four winds, you shall have this extra day every four years, and then everyone will remember the great leap Prince Orlando and I took on his magic ribbon of golden light to challenge the Wizard of the Crystal Lake. We will call every fourth year Leap Year."

Everyone cheered. February, who had been envious of the other horses, now glowed with pride, and he too wanted to make a speech, but he didn't, because horses can't talk.

And so the king and his new wife and Prince Orlando and the lovely Princess Rosalinda, she of the Four Winds, lived happy lives as the years passed and as the winds blew cold and warm. The castle was safe; the calendar was complete, since now the year had twelve months and every month had its gift of days and every year had 365 days with one day added for Leap Year; and the Moon Horses, who were only borrowed were returned to the Man in the Moon. Rosalinda went with Orlando on the flight to the moon, where she met the smiling

old fellow with the bald head and the crazy laughter; she admired the view of the earth and said she liked nothing better than traveling to new places. But after returning to the earth, the young prince discovered that he had shot his last arrow. He could no longer remember where to find the Mound of Ancient Earth and the Cave of Hidden Light, but he told himself that he had followed the old woman's advice: working, and using his imagination, and going on exciting adventures: and now married to the lovely princess, he found happiness. So he and his bride decided it would be sensible to travel by coach now and then but to spend more time together in the castle, where they could now raise a family and tell their children about all the marvelous things that happened to them, just as I've told you.

THE END

Made in the USA
Middletown, DE
13 January 2017